The N

Arthur A. Levine Books   An imprint of Scholastic inc.

ight Eater

Ana
Juan

At the edge of every day,

the Night Eater ran behind the moon.

And as he ran, the Night Eater gobbled

up the darkness. When he stopped, his

friends continued on without him,

and he rested on the top of

the highest mountain.

The Night Eater ate every kind

of night: cloudy nights as light

and sweet as cotton candy

and deep black nights

that tasted like

bitter chocolate.

His favorite kind of night was bright and clear.

The stars were like bubbles of gas, tickling his nose as they went down.

Through the
wee hours
of the morning
the Night Eater
ran. . . .

From the mountains to the sea, from the sea to the desert ...

. . . leaving his friend the sun

the pleasure of saying "Good morning" to everyone.

And so time passed, as night followed day, and day followed night.

Until one day,

the moon looked back

at his friend and said,

"Oh, my! Night Eater,

you've gotten a bit

LARGE, haven't you?"

The Night Eater was shocked.

And then embarrassed.

"Then I won't eat

another bite of night," he said.

And he folded his arms

and sat down.

At first it wasn't a problem.
People woke from their sleep
and discovered things they
had never before imagined.
Nocturnal animals and
perfumed flowers,
whose petals opened
only at night.

But after a while without
the sun, it got cold.

People switched on their heaters,

even though it was summertime.

Faces grew pale and night flowers died.

Even they needed daylight to survive.

The sun grew restless, trapped behind the
mountain. And the moon grew tired
of shining his weak light.

Children looked up at the sky and cried,

"Where is the Night Eater?

Why won't he come?"

The Night Eater
opened his mouth
to answer, and in
slipped a sliver of star.

It was so good, and so tasty, he forgot why he had refused to nibble.

And soon he was off and running again.

And his friends ran happily with him.

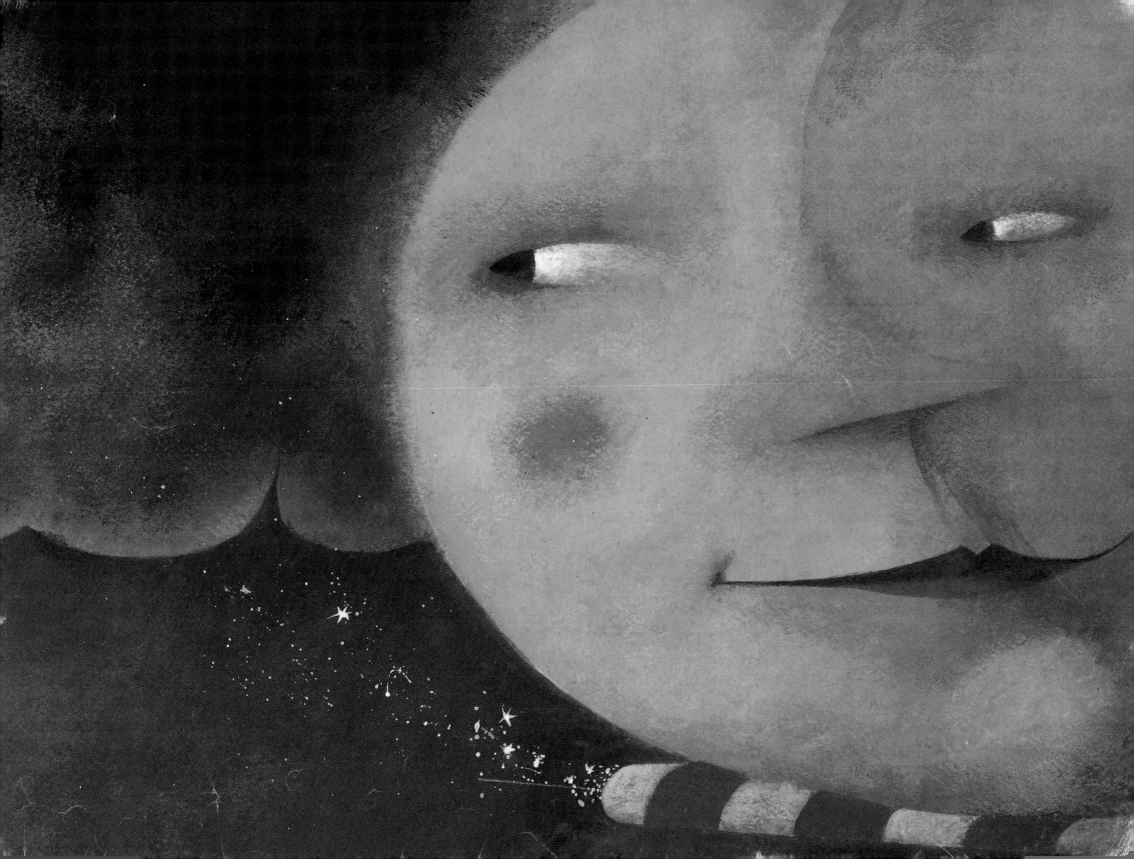

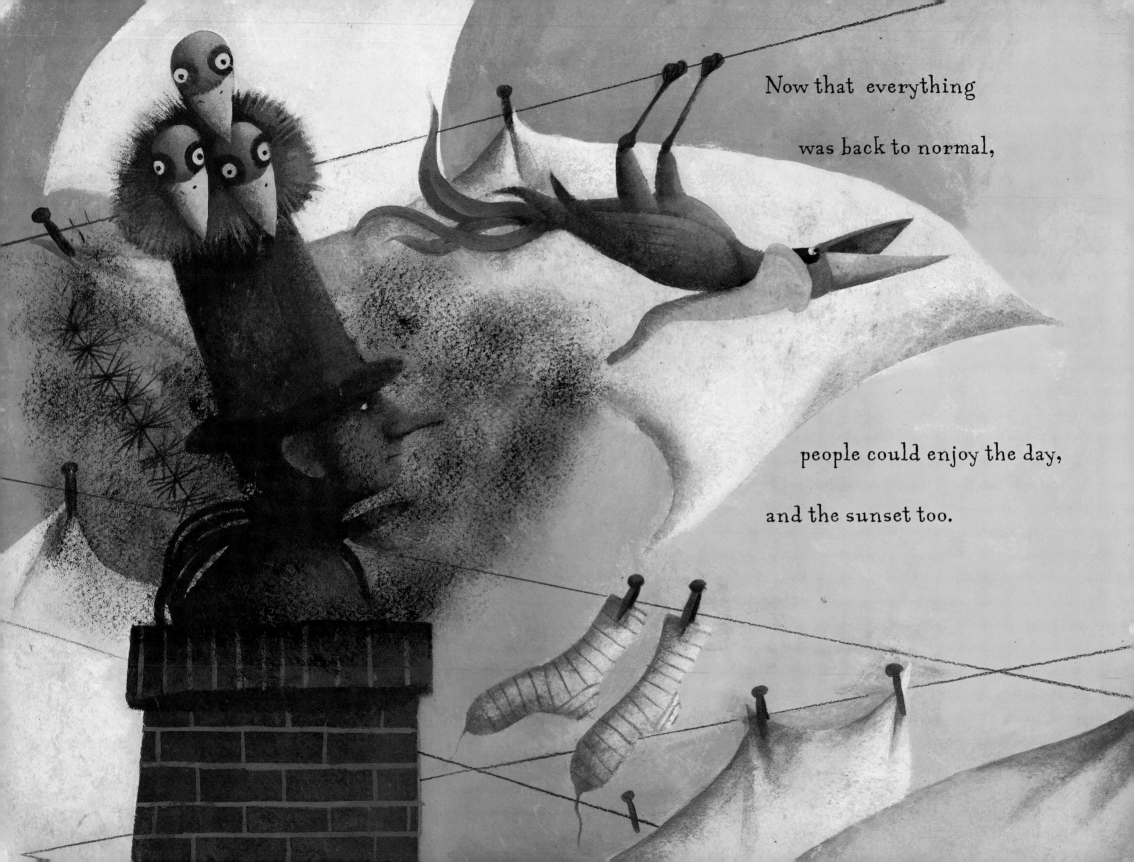

Now that everything

was back to normal,

people could enjoy the day,

and the sunset too.

Followed by a night

that was filled

with stars,

and a dawn

radiant with sun.

Even the clouds

couldn't spoil things.

As for the Night Eater,

he went back to his rounds,

running behind the delicious darkness.

And afterward, resting on his mountaintop,

he saved a little piece in his hat,

so he'd always remember

the sweetness of night.

For Matz, for looking after my days and nights.

LIBRARY OF CONGRESS CATALOGING-IN-PUBLICATION DATA

Juan, Ana.
The Night Eater / by Ana Juan.— 1st ed.   p. cm.
Summary: The Night Eater, who brings each new day by gobbling up the darkness,
decides he is too fat and stops eating, with dire consequences.
ISBN 0-439-48891-5
[1. Night—Fiction.] I. Title. PZ7.J8575Ni 2004 [E]—dc22 2003020197

10 9 8 7 6 5 4 3 2 1   04 05 06 07 08
The art was created by using acrylics and wax on paper.
The jacket title type was hand-lettered by Ana Juan.
The text type was set in 24-pt. Aunt Mildred.
The display type was set in Dandelion.
Book design by Marijka Kostiw
First edition, October 2004
Printed in Singapore 46